Some other books by Margaret Nash

CLASS 1 ON THE MOVE

ENOUGH IS ENOUGH
THE HAUNTED CANAL
RAT SATURDAY

Margaret Nash

CLASS 1 SPELLS TROUBLE

Illustrated by Julie Park

PUFFIN BOOKS

For Jean P., Jean W., Diane, Jan, Penn, Ida and Sybil.

PUFFIN BOOKS

Published by the Penguin Group
Penguin Books Ltd, 27 Wrights Lane, London W8 5TZ, England
Penguin Books USA Inc., 375 Hudson Street, New York, New York 10014, USA
Penguin Books Australia Ltd, Ringwood, Victoria, Australia
Penguin Books Canada Ltd, 10 Alcorn Avenue, Toronto, Ontario, Canada M4V 3B2
Penguin Books (NZ) Ltd, 182–190 Wairau Road, Auckland 10, New Zealand

Penguin Books Ltd, Registered Offices: Harmondsworth, Middlesex, England

First published by Viking 1990
Published in Puffin Books 1992
10 9 8 7 6 5

Text copyright © Margaret Nash, 1990
Illustrations copyright © Julie Park, 1990
All rights reserved

The moral right of the author has been asserted

Printed in England by Clays Ltd, St Ives plc
Filmset in Linotron Baskerville

0140342249

Contents

You Can't Afford to Take the Risk!

"Enough's enough, Jeremy Price," said Miss Boswell. "Stop showing off and sit down." Jeremy Price, who was slapping a roll of Plasticine on his desk, sat down.

"And that's enough of that, Andy Billings." Andy Billings had just fired a Plasticine cannon-ball off his ruler at Mary Moss. He stopped. Sally Pontin was watching him, and thinking how silly he was.

You see, Sally Pontin was in a grown-up mood today. Her plaits were pinned on top of her head and that always made her feel at least two years older. It also meant Jamie Smart couldn't pull her plaits. She looked at the large lump of Plasticine on her desk. Miss Boswell was walking round the classroom, making sure that everyone had started making something. She hadn't.

"Rather a lot of baskets and snakes," said Miss Boswell. "Can't someone make an animal?" Class 1 groaned. Sally Pontin didn't groan. It was

babyish. Yes, she'd make an animal – a pink animal. She'd make a pink pig, that's what. She rolled the Plasticine into a ball, and added two pig ears, and four rather wobbly pig legs, and stuck two bits of wax crayon into the head for eyes.

Miss Boswell's footsteps were coming nearer. They were making a lovely "titter-toeing" sound on the hard floor. Sally liked the noise. She was definitely going to wear high heels when she grew up. Miss Boswell stopped by Sally's desk.

"Now there's a girl who's trying," Miss Boswell said. Sally shuffled importantly and began rolling out a thin piece of Plasticine. Jamie Smart looked at her and wrinkled his nose.

"We are not supposed to make any more snakes," he said.

"It's not a snake. It's a pig's

tail," said Sally. She turned
away and started to curl it. She
stuck the tail on the pig and
leaned back on her chair to
admire it.

"Caw, is that a pig?" shouted
Paul King. "What a big bottom
it's got."

"Like yours," said Sally
Pontin and picked up the pig
and went out to show it to Miss
Boswell. Miss Boswell showed
the pig to the whole class, and
they admired it.

"Put it somewhere safe," said

Miss Boswell. "But do put it out of the sunshine. Sunshine does funny things to Plasticine animals and we don't want to take any risks." Sally looked at Miss Boswell and was just going to ask what risks they might be taking when Miss Boswell stood up and clapped her hands.

"Now, everyone into the story corner." Class 1 cheered and rushed on to the square of carpet near the big window. They didn't often have stories in the morning. Miss Boswell walked over to the story corner and sat on her special chair. She crossed one long leg over the other long leg.

"Quiet please, Class 1," she said and opened her book.

Usually, at this point, the class fell silent, but not today. The sun was streaming in through the window and it was getting hot. Julie Parker got an itch and kept squirming around. Mary Moss fiddled with her shoe

buckle and Sally Pontin just couldn't concentrate. She kept looking at her pink pig over by the blackboard. She was pleased with him. He did look good. He looked almost real. It must be the wax eyes glinting in the sun which made him look real, Sally thought.

It was getting very warm. Everyone was shuffling. Andy Billings yawned. He always seemed to yawn when he ran out of chewing-gum.

"Stop yawning," said Miss Boswell. "It's catching. We'll all be yawning soon." Andy shut his mouth. Miss Boswell

went on reading. Paul King
yawned. Sally yawned and
looked at her pig. The sun was
just creeping over his feet. Then
he yawned. Sally blinked and
stared. Yes, he was doing it
again. And he seemed to be
swaying, swaying and yawning.
All four of his feet were in a pool
of sunshine now.

"Miss Boswell, look at my pig!" But Miss Boswell was enjoying reading the story and didn't look. Maybe she didn't even hear Sally. But the other children did.

"It's leaning over," said Mary Moss.

"It must be the sun," said Julie Parker.

"Now settle down, Class 1," said Miss Boswell. Nobody settled down. Instead, most of them jumped up. The pig was growing now. It surely was. And what's more, it was growing quickly.

"It's as big as a real pig – well, a piglet," said Jeremy Price. "Look, Miss Boswell!" Jeremy Price had a very loud voice. Miss Boswell stopped reading and looked. She jumped up and the book landed on the floor with a thump.

"Goodness! It's the sun. Quick, we must get it out of the sun. Stand back everyone."

Miss Boswell pushed through Class 1 and rushed towards the pig but the pig suddenly took a step forward, then another one, and then waddled away, its big bottom swaying. It was going towards the door. Jeremy Price stood in the doorway, but the pig squealed and squeezed between his legs.

"Squashy stuff, Plasticine," said Miss Boswell. The pig ran down the corridor. Class 1 ran after it. The pig got up speed as it went. It pushed into the secretary's office where Mrs Dilley was sitting behind neat piles of school-dinner money.

The pig knocked the table and the coins rolled everywhere. The pig snorted and ran out. It pushed into the headmaster's office. Mr Pringle was studying a book and did not see it. The pig came out.

"No need to tell the headmaster. He's far too busy to bother about pigs," said Miss Boswell, and she quietly shut the door. The pig ran into the kitchen. Cook was just sharpening her knife.

"Bacon!" she yelled. The pig honked and rushed towards her. Cook got up on the sink and clung to the towel rail.

"Oh, I do wish we'd noticed the sun," said Miss Boswell. "We should have put it in a cupboard where the sun couldn't get it." Sally Pontin tried to grab the pig but missed and the pig pushed over the waste bin and rushed under the table. Sally skidded on the mess

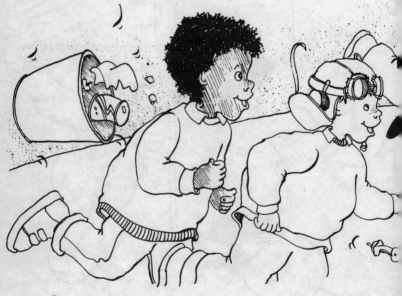

and had to grab hold of the
table leg, and the pig ran out of
the doorway. Everyone was
rushing past her, following the
pig. It went into the

playground. Then suddenly it turned. Its ears hung over its eyes like droopy flags.

"My uncle was once killed by a pig," said Julie Parker. "He told me so."

"How could he talk if he was dead?" said Jamie Smart and Julie's face went bright red and she said he was nearly killed. The pig moved forward and grunted at Mary Moss. Mary Moss screamed.

"We'll have to lasso it," said Jamie Smart. "I know where there's a piece of old rope."

"Don't be silly," said Miss Boswell. "You can't lasso

Plasticine. Chase it back into the classroom."

"Shoo, shoo, go on," shouted Class 1. The pig *did* go on. It went on round the dustbins, round the corner of Class 2 who all rushed to the window and waved, on down to the school playing-field, back past the

boiler house, and finally stopped
by a heap of sludgy mud where
the workmen had been.

"Now enough really is
enough," said Miss Boswell to
the pig. But enough was not
enough for the pig. It gave a
loud grunt and dived right into
the middle of the mud.

"Pigs adore rolling in mud," said Jamie Smart. "We'll never get it out now." The pig did enjoy it. He wallowed around sending the squelchy stuff everywhere. Andy Billings got a mud-splattered face which Julie Parker thought very funny until some landed on her new shoes. Jamie Smart got a lump of mud down his neck and Andy Billings didn't dare blow his gum out in case some mud went in his mouth.

"Hey, steady on," said Miss Boswell and she stepped towards the mud and skidded. But the pig did not steady on.

He got even wilder. In fact, he got so wild that soon he was almost covered in the mud. Then gradually his grunts got fewer.

"I expect the mud's cooling

32

him down," said Miss Boswell.
"It was getting overheated
which made him wild." She
looked at her mud-splattered
legs and sighed.

"He's getting smaller," said
Mary Moss.

"Oh yes, he is," said Sally Pontin. Class 1 quietly stared down into the mud. The lump gradually got smaller and smaller. There were no grunts any more, just the odd glugging sound as an air bubble rose to the surface.

"Caw," said Jamie Smart. "You can hardly see him now." It was true. There was just a tiny hump in the mud.

"Right," said Miss Boswell. "That's cooled him down now. Time he went back in the Plasticine tin." She rolled up her sleeve and slowly reached into the mud. She drew out a grey and pink mottled lump of rather slimy Plasticine, rolled it into a ball and gave it to Andy Billings.

"Put it away in the Plasticine tin, Andy. I think we've all had enough of Plasticine for today.

And remember Class 1, *never ever* put Plasticine animals in the sunshine. You just don't know what might happen. You can't afford to take the risk!"

The Hallowe'en Witch

Paul King was the first to see the witch. Miss Boswell was just in the middle of saying good morning when the witch rose out of the mist and hovered over the school playing-field. She was looking towards Class 1.

"Look," yelled Paul King,
"look, there's a witch!"
Everyone in Class 1 turned to
look.

"Where, where?" said Julie Parker, standing on a chair.

"Where?" shouted Sally Pontin, and she rushed to the window to see. But the witch wasn't there any more. The mist had moved and the witch had gone. But she had been there. Paul King was certain of it. He said so.

"Go on," said Jeremy Price. "Don't be daft." He liked to be the one to see things first, did Jeremy Price.

"Well, it *is* Hallowe'en tonight after all," said Miss Boswell. She touched the half-made turnip lantern on her desk and sighed. There were piles of paper spiders, string cobwebs and black cats still to be hung up before Class 1's Hallowe'en party.

"I couldn't see anyone," said Julie Parker, and she climbed down from her chair as noisily as she dared.

The next time Paul King saw the witch was in assembly. She was skulking in the shadows at the back of the overhead projector. He nudged Julie

Parker, and whispered, "Look, the witch is behind you." Julie turned round but she knocked into Andy Billings and he fell against Jamie Smart. Both boys fell down.

"What is going on, Class 1?"
said Miss Boswell in her bossy
voice, and she turned off the
projector. The witch
disappeared. Paul King was
cross. He couldn't tell anyone
else now. The witch had gone
again. But at break time a
crowd gathered round.

"Tell us about this witch,"
they said. "Go on." Sally Pontin
came up blowing bubble stuff
through a hoop, followed by
Jamie Smart kicking a Coke tin.

"Well, she didn't have a hat.
She had straggly hair and a
hooked nose," Paul King told
them. "And she looked
greenish," he added. Jeremy
Price did one of his big silly
laughs and shied a stone at the
dustbin. Mary Moss bit her lip.

"Rubbish," said Sally Pontin
and blew a bubble right in front
of Paul King's face. It got
larger and larger until she
jerked it off the hoop; it then

hovered over them like a
delicate ball laced with pretty
colours. But as Paul King
looked, the colours altered until
there, inside the bubble, looking
out at him, was a face – a
witch's face.

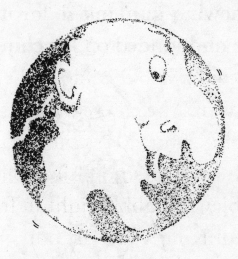

"Crikey," he said. "The witch again."

"Where, where?" shouted the others but the bubble suddenly burst and that was the end of the witch.

"I didn't see anything," said Andy Billings, and he stretched his chewing-gum out so far it broke and landed on his chin.

"Neither did I," said Jamie Smart. "He's making it up."

"I thought I saw something," said Sally Pontin, "but it was all wobbly." She put the top back on the bubble stuff and put it away.

"Well, *you'd* be all wobbly if you were inside a bubble," said Paul King. "She was there all right."

Paul told Miss Boswell about the witch.

"What? You've seen her again?"

"Yes," said Paul. "She was inside Sally's bubble."

"She wasn't," said Julie Parker.

"She was," said Paul King and pulled a face at her. Miss Boswell sat down on her table top, her high-heeled shoes clinking gently against the table leg.

"Did anyone else see her?" asked Miss Boswell.

"No," said Class 1.

"Sally did," said Paul.

"No, I didn't," said Sally Pontin. "I've changed my

mind." She put the end of her plait in her mouth and shuffled some papers on her desk.

"Now enough's enough," said Miss Boswell. "We've got to settle down to some hard sums before we can put up the decorations for our party." Settling down meant a lot of groaning and shuffling to Class 1 but they tried.

Paul King sighed. He felt odd, sort of shivery. He was sure there was a witch still about. But where? The mist on the playing-field had gone. It was being replaced by streaks of weak Autumn sunshine. He looked at the witches' hats Class 1 had made. They were standing on top of the paper cupboard. They all had moons and stars on them, all except for one. This one was plain black and looked as if it hadn't been finished. Suddenly, he saw it move – at least he thought he did, and then he wasn't sure.

"Miss Boswell," he called

out. "Can we wear our witches' hats while we do our sums?"

"Oh yes, Miss, let's," chorused Class 1. Miss Boswell clapped her hands to silence them.

"All right."

There was a rush to the paper cupboard. Paul King got there first. He made a grab for the plain black hat. It wasn't moving after all. It was still, and it fitted him perfectly.

"Now, on with your sums," said Miss Boswell.

The class settled down. Paul looked at the rows of hats in front of him all pointing forwards. He began adding up. The sums weren't difficult. What was Miss Boswell talking about? He went out to have them marked. Every sum got a tick.

"Well done, Paul King," announced Miss Boswell. "Now there's a boy who's tried, Class 1." Paul King swaggered back to his place. Sally Pontin pulled his sleeve.

"How did you do it? They're

so blooming hard. I'm stuck."

"I think it's the hat," said Paul. "I think it's got special powers."

"Don't be silly," she said.

"Shh," said Miss Boswell. "Some of us are trying to work." Paul King pulled the hat down over his ears. I wish I didn't have to do any more sums, he thought.

"Paul King," called out Miss Boswell. "Would you like to come and finish the turnip lantern?" Would he! Paul had his books put away before you could say "Hallowe'en".

It was hard work scraping out the inside of the turnip. I do wish it was easier, he thought.

The hat seemed to tighten slightly around his ears and suddenly it was easier, much easier. He carved two triangles for eyes and put a large smiling mouth in the turnip. Miss Boswell was delighted and held it up for Class 1 to see, then she went to the cupboard to get a candle for it, but she came out without one.

"I'm sorry, Class 1. I just can't find the candles." Class 1 groaned and pulled faces.

"But we must have it lit up," said Julie Parker. Paul looked at Miss Boswell's desk. He couldn't believe it.

"Er, Miss Boswell, look –
there's one on your desk. It's
just behind you."

"Well, I never," said Miss
Boswell. "It must have been
there all the time." Class 1
cheered. Paul felt his head
tingle. It must be the power of
the hat.

"Well done, hat," he said, gently stroking its brim. Jamie Smart heard. He was still struggling with his sums.

"Give me the hat," he demanded. Paul King rammed it down over Jamie's head. But Jamie Smart didn't have time to test it for the dinner bell sounded.

"Oh, dear," said Miss Boswell. "We still haven't got our decorations up. We'll never be ready for the party." Class 1 took off their hats and jostled back to the paper cupboard with them. Paul King grabbed the hat back off Jamie Smart.

"Take it then, baby," said Jamie Smart. "Go on."

"Who believes in witches?" said Andy Billings, and cackled loudly.

"Well, I wish there was one about," said Sally Pontin. "I'm beginning to get into a spooky mood. It's nice." She took the hat off Paul and put it on her head and jigged around.

"I wish the witch would trim up our room," she said. "It doesn't look like Hallowe'en." Mary Moss shivered. Paul grabbed the hat back and stuck it on top of the paper cupboard.

"I'll look for her after dinner," he said.

He did look. He looked everywhere; behind dustbins, over walls, even at the back of the boiler house, but nowhere could he find a witch.

"Told you," said Jeremy Price. "There isn't a witch." He kicked his apple core over the school roof. Paul shrugged. The

whistle blew and they drifted
into school. Miss Boswell was
standing at the classroom door.

"Come in slowly, children."
Class 1 immediately hurried.

They gasped as they saw their classroom. Spiders were hanging from the ceiling, cobwebs were draped across corners of the room. On every child's desk stood a black cardboard cat, and on Miss Boswell's desk stood a beautiful turnip lantern with triangular eyes and a glowing orange smile.

"Oh, who did that?" said Julie Parker. Sally Pontin and Paul King looked at one another.

"The witch," they said together. Miss Boswell smiled and said it might have been.

"Go on," said Jeremy Price. "There is no witch. It must have been you, Miss Boswell." Miss Boswell smiled.

"I couldn't have done all this on my own, could I?" she said.

"That black hat's gone," said Mary Moss quietly. Everyone looked at the paper cupboard; everyone except Paul King. He'd just seen something flick past the window. He rushed towards the window.

"Look," he yelled. "The witch!" Class 1 hurtled up behind him. Sure enough, high

up in the pale Autumn clouds
was the rough shape of a witch
– a witch without a hat. As they
looked another cloud rolled
along and joined it. Then the
whole thing re-adjusted to form
the shape of a perfect
Hallowe'en witch wearing a
very pointed hat. Miss Boswell
tottered back on her high heels,
and waved. The whole of
Class 1 waved.

"I reckon she came back for her hat," said Miss Boswell, and she smiled her special smile which usually meant she knew something Class 1 didn't.

"Yes," said Class 1, and even Jeremy Price dared not say no. He looked behind into the spooky, glowing classroom.

"Come on," he said, "let's start the party!"

Mary Moss's Balloon

Mary Moss and Sally Pontin rushed through the school gate. They didn't usually go to school on Saturdays but today was different. There were stalls in the school playing-field and bunting and banners. Music was playing and children were having donkey rides. Yes, it certainly was different. Jamie Smart came running up to them.

"I'm off to buy an elephant," he said.

"What?" asked Sally Pontin.

"An elephant, a white one. There's a white elephant stall over there." He laughed, then trumpeted loudly and lumbered off with his arm dangling from his face, pretending to be an elephant. The music stopped. The headmaster's voice came through the loudspeakers.

"Welcome to the fête everybody, and can I just remind you that Class 1's balloon race is at half past three. It's sure to be fun. Meanwhile, enjoy yourselves.

All proceeds go towards the new
computer." Some people made
a big thing of clapping. Julie
Parker came up to them. She
couldn't clap. She was too busy
with her dripping ice-cream.

"The balloon man's arrived,"
she said. "I've seen him."

Class 1 had been studying
real balloons, balloons with
baskets that carried people high
in the sky and over the fields.
They'd all made baskets out of
yoghurt pots and Miss Boswell's
friend, the balloon man, was
coming with gas-filled balloons
for their baskets. Mary Moss
had painted her basket pink.
She was going to choose a pink

balloon. She was so busy
thinking about pink balloons
that she bumped into Jamie
Smart's pink candyfloss and got
it on her face. It felt horrid –
like a spider's web.

"Oh, look, there's Gypsy Bright Eyes," said Sally Pontin. "I must have my fortune told." She went towards a grey-looking tent and peeped inside.

"Go on," said Julie Parker, "and I'll come too." With that, she pushed Sally inside. Mary Moss wasn't keen. She stayed outside, hoping they wouldn't be long. Then she saw her mother among the crowds and ran across to her.

Mrs Moss was standing in front of the cake stall, trying to decide what to buy.

"Oh, look at that beautiful

cake," said Mary. Right in the
middle of the stall on a large
silver plate stood a chocolate
cake. It was all frothed up
round the edges with lime green
cream and decorated with blue
bows and chocolate roses. It
was enormous.

"That's a gâteau," said Mrs Moss. "I certainly can't afford that. Besides, it looks sort of special, as though it is there for a purpose." Instead, she bought six dull-looking currant buns.

Mary Moss left her mum talking to old Mrs Chatter, and went to look for Sally and Julie. She found them both laughing outside Gypsy Bright Eyes' tent.

"It's Jeremy Price's mum in there, covered in tassels and curtain rings," they said. "She said we're both going to be ballet dancers when we grow up." Julie arched her hands above her head, ready to do a

twirl, only she lost her balance
and fell against the tent. It
wobbled dangerously around
Gypsy Bright Eyes, and they
had to run away.

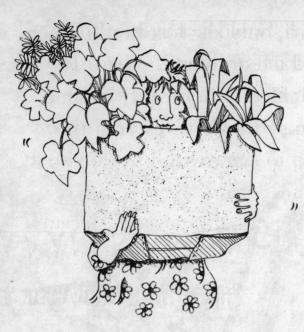

Suddenly, Miss Boswell
appeared carrying a large box
of plants. She looked like
something off the plant stall
herself, did Miss Boswell. She
was dressed in a very flowery
frock and was wearing daisy
earrings.

"I should get over to the balloon stall now," she said. "Most of Class 1 are there already." Then she hurried on with the others following closely behind.

"That's my basket," Jeremy Price was saying, pointing to one with a gorilla on the front.

"I'm having a red balloon, red for danger," said Jamie Smart.

"I'll have yellow so that I'll be able to see it when it's high in the sky," said Julie Parker.

"Mind you don't get it muddled up with the sun," said Andy Billings and blew his

chewing-gum out far enough to
stick on the back of Julie's neck.
She turned round and pulled a
face at him.

There were no pink balloons.
Mary Moss was disappointed.

"Have this white one,"
suggested the balloon man.

"It's special. Look – it's got a
face on." It did look rather nice.
It had big eyes and a straight
mouth.

"All right," said Mary and
took hold of it.

"My balloon's going all the way to Australia," said Julie. "I can tell." And she patted it proudly.

"Mine might go into space," said Paul King. "I'm going to put a beetle in the basket just in case. It will be the first beetle in space."

"I wonder where you're going," said Mary Moss, looking at her balloon.

"Nowhere special," said Jeremy Price. "White balloons never do any good. They're boring things." Miss Boswell heard him.

"Enough's enough of that sort of talk," she said. "None of the balloons will go far. The weight of the baskets will hold them down rather, but we'll see. One or two might surprise us. Now, are you all holding your balloons? Ready?" Mr Pringle's voice boomed out round the field.

"Class 1 are ready to launch their balloons. Is everyone watching?" Everyone turned to face the balloon stall.

"Ready then, Class 1," said Mr Pringle. "When I fire this cap gun let go of your balloons." He counted down from three. "Three, two, one" – BANG.

Class 1 watched as their
balloons and baskets rose. Mary
Moss's balloon seemed to shoot
upwards.

"See," she said to Jeremy
Price. "White balloons are
good. And ones with faces are
special anyway. The man said
so." Julie Parker started
jumping up and down and
shouting at hers.

"Go on, go on," she yelled. Her balloon was as high as the school roof now but it didn't rise any more. "Go on, go on," she yelled, but it didn't. It dropped slightly and wafted down towards the chimney pot, then sort of shuffled itself on to the chimney pot and stayed there. "Stupid thing," she shouted. "Get up!" But it didn't.

"Oh, no," said Andy Billings, and he rushed towards the cherry tree. His balloon was stuck in its branches. He got it out but it only did a couple of twirls, then softened and flopped down to earth in a very disappointing way.

"First casualty," said Miss Boswell. "Never mind, Andy." Andy cracked his gum loudly to show he didn't mind.

Jamie Smart's red-for-danger balloon came down and landed on a bush. He laughed loudly, picked up a stone, and was just about to enjoy bursting it properly when Miss Boswell tapped him on the shoulder and told him not to.

No more came down for a while, then gradually they all started falling. But Mary Moss couldn't see hers. Paul King's came down and landed on Julie Parker's head and his beetle fell out. She shrieked and Paul told her she could have the beetle as the balloon had not gone into space and it wasn't going to be a space beetle after all. Some balloons landed in the next field. Sally's did. Mary Moss still couldn't see hers. She told Sally Pontin.

"Perhaps it's so high it's out of sight," said Sally, and linked her arm through Mary's arm. "That must be the reason."

One by one all the balloons came back. Everyone clapped and cheered as they landed.

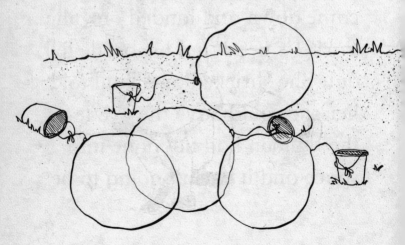

Mary still couldn't see hers. She
told Miss Boswell.

"White is difficult to see in
the sky," said Miss Boswell.
Everyone waited, then suddenly
an announcement was made by
the balloon man.

"Right everyone, I expect you're all waiting to hear the results of the balloon race. All the balloons have come back except for one – the white one which did go high, and as I can't see it . . ." He paused and looked up into the sky, ". . . I think it has probably gone the furthest."

Mary Moss clenched her fists with excitement. Was she going to be the winner? She stood on tiptoe to get a better view of the man.

"So would the owner of the white balloon please step forward?" said the balloon

man. Mary eagerly pushed her
way to the front, but suddenly
there was a scuffling. Someone
else was pushing through the
knot of people. There was a
jingling of jewellery and bells. It
was Gypsy Bright Eyes.

"Hold on, hold on," she said. "I know exactly where the balloon is!" There was silence. Gypsy Bright Eyes touched her forehead and swayed her hips. "I see it," she said. "I see it in soft surroundings." People started giggling. Jeremy Price's face went red. His mother did rather tend to overdo things.

"Where, where?" said Paul King, but Gypsy Bright Eyes would not be rushed. She looked down, touched her forehead again, then looked up.

"I see it resting,' she said.

"It's not burst then," said Mary Moss.

"No, no, it is quite safe." The
balloon man was scratching his
head and looking upwards.
Miss Boswell was biting her lip
and trying not to laugh.

"Over there," boomed Gypsy
Bright Eyes. "There it lies."
Everyone turned round.

"Where?" said Mary Moss,
and then she saw it. It *was*
resting. It *was* certainly safe,
and it *was* in soft surroundings –
cream ones. It was sitting right

on top of the prize gâteau on the
cake stall, among the blue bows
and chocolate roses. And what
is more, the balloon was not soft
and soggy like some. No – it
was as round and firm as when
it was launched.

Everyone laughed and clapped
and rushed over to see it.

"But what can we do with the
cake, our prize gâteau?" said
Miss Boswell. "It's ruined."

"Eat it, eat it," yelled
Class 1.

And as no one said no, Sally Pontin ran off to the staff room to get paper plates, and Miss Boswell fetched a knife and cut the cake into small pieces. There was enough for all the children in Class 1, and Miss Boswell and her friend the balloon man, and the headmaster. There was even some cake left over for the parents too.

In the middle of the "grand eating" a man from the newspaper came to take a photo of the fête. Everyone said Mary Moss should be photographed with the balloon. And she was.

She put on a nice big smile for the camera man.

But the amazing thing was, that when the photograph came out, she wasn't the only one smiling. No, the balloon was smiling too. Its straight mouth seemed to have turned up at the corners and it had a smile as big as Mary's on its face.

"Well, after all," explained Mary Moss, "Miss Boswell's friend, the balloon man, *did* say the balloon was special, and it was!"